For Sarah and Miranda Crane and all their friends
L. N.

To my wonderful family, and to Heather's wonderful family
L. C.

Special thanks to Tzivia Gover, original publisher,
and Diana Souza, original illustrator.

Published 2015 by Walker Books Ltd
87 Vauxhall Walk, London SE11 5HJ

This edition published 2016

4 6 8 10 9 7 5

This book has been typeset in Godlike

Printed in China

British Library Cataloguing in Publication Data:
a catalogue record for this book is available from the British Library

ISBN 978-1-4063-6555-9

www.walker.co.uk

Heather Has Two Mummies

Lesléa Newman   illustrated by Laura Cornell

WALKER BOOKS
AND SUBSIDIARIES
LONDON · BOSTON · SYDNEY · AUCKLAND

Heather lives in a little house with a big apple tree in the front garden and lots of tall grass in the back garden.

Heather's favourite number is two.
She has two arms, two legs, two eyes,
two ears, two hands and two feet.

Heather has two pets:
a ginger-coloured cat named Gingernut
and a big black dog named Midnight.

Heather also has two mummies:
Mama Jane and Mama Kate.

Mama Kate is a doctor. She has two
stethoscopes so she and Heather can
listen to each other's heartbeats.

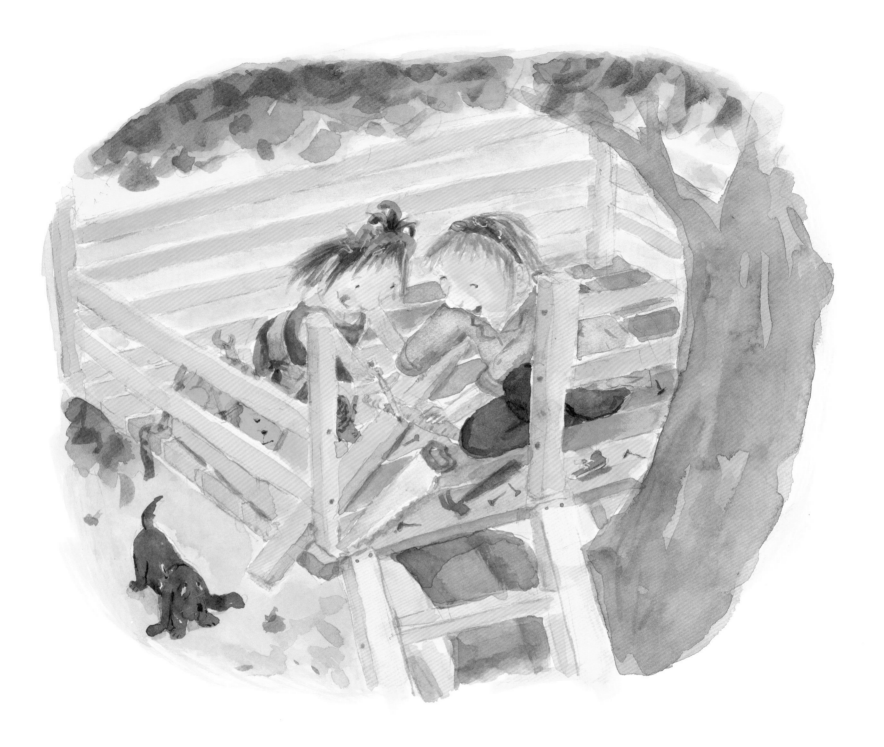

Mama Jane is a carpenter. She has two
hammers so she and Heather can build
things together.

Heather and her mummies have lots of fun together. On sunny days, they go to the park.

On rainy days, they stay inside and
bake biscuits. Heather likes to eat two
ginger nuts and drink a big glass of milk.

One day, Mama Kate and Mama Jane tell Heather that they have a surprise for her. "You're going to start school next week!" Mama Kate says.

"There'll be lots of other kids to play with and a teacher named Ms Molly," adds Mama Jane.

"Can Midnight and Gingernut come, too?" asks Heather.

"No, they have to stay at home," Mama Jane says.

"But you can take two special things with you," says Mama Kate.

Heather chooses her favourite blue blanket to rest with at nap time and her favourite red cup to drink from at snack time.

Soon the big day arrives, and
Mama Kate and Mama Jane take
Heather to her new school.

There are so many things to play with! Heather sees
building blocks, dressing-up clothes, crayons and paint.
Heather also sees a big round table for snack time and
a quiet cosy corner for nap time.

While Mama Jane and Mama Kate talk to Ms Molly,
Heather puts two puzzles together all by herself.

Soon it's time for Mama Jane and Mama Kate to leave. They kiss Heather goodbye, and Heather cries. But only a bit.

Heather has lots of fun at her new school. She builds a tower out of building blocks ...

and dresses up like a firefighter.

She drinks apple juice from her favourite red cup at snack time and rests in the quiet corner with her favourite blue blanket at nap time.

After nap time, all the children sit in a circle while
Ms Molly reads them a story about a boy whose father
is a veterinarian.

"Who knows what a veterinarian is?" asks Ms Molly.

"I do! My mummy is a veterinarian," Juan says.
"A veterinarian is an animal doctor."

The good doctor uses
his stethoscope gently
on little Buster.

Dr Katz must be
careful that his patient
does not eat the tongue
depressor.

"My daddy is a people doctor!" shouts David.

"My mummy is a people doctor, too!" Heather shouts even louder.

"What does your daddy do?" David asks Heather.

"I don't have a daddy," Heather says. She looks round the circle and wonders, *Am I the only one here who doesn't have a daddy?*

"I have an idea," Ms Molly says. "Let's all draw pictures of our families."

Juan draws his mummy, daddy
and big brother, Carlos.

Miriam draws her mummy and her
sister, Rachel, playing in the park.

Stacy draws her daddy and her papa
reading her stories.

Joshua hangs up the picture he drew
of his mummy and his stepfather dropping
him off at his daddy's house.

Emily tapes up the picture she drew of her grandma and their two puppies, Henry and Charlie.

David straightens out the picture he drew of the day his mummy and daddy brought his new sister, Veronica, home.

Ms Molly looks at all the pictures. "It doesn't matter how many mummies or how many daddies your family has," Ms Molly says. "It doesn't matter if your family has sisters or brothers or cousins or grandmas or grandpas or uncles or aunts."

"Each family is special. The most important thing about a family is that all the people in it love one another."

Soon Heather's first day of school is over. When Mama Kate and Mama Jane arrive to pick her up, Heather shows them all the pictures.

"Is that me?" Mama Kate asks, pointing at Heather's picture.

"And is that me?" Mama Jane asks, pointing, too.

"This is the mummy I love the best," Heather says, pointing at her picture. "And *this* is the mummy I love the best," Heather says, pointing again.

Mama Kate and Mama Jane both laugh as Heather gives each of them two kisses. Then she takes their hands and they all head home.